Honeypot Hill

← To the City

Saffron Thimble's
Sewing Shop

The Orchards

Paddle Steamer
Quay

Aunt
Marigold's
General
Store

Lavender Valley
Garden Centre

Healing House and Garden

The Worthingtons' House

Lavender Lake

Melody
Maker's
Music Shop

Bumble Bee's Teashop

Lavender Lake
School of Dance

SCHOOL

Hedgerows Hotel
Where Mimosa lives

Peppermint
Pond

Rosehip School

Summer Meadow

Christmas Corner

Wildspice Woods

Honeysuckle Cottage
Poppy's House

Forget-Me-Not Cottage
Grandpa's House and Office

Poppy Field

N
W   E
S

Honeypot Cottage
Honey and Granny Bumble's House

Blossom
Bakehouse

Cornsilk Castle
and Courtyard

Village Hall

Sage's
Vet Surgery

Post Office

River Swan

Beehive
Beauty Salon

Barley Farm
The Meadowsweets' House

Riverside
Stables

Honeypot Hill
Railway Station

To Camomile Cove
via Periwinkle Lane

Check out Princess Poppy's brilliant website:

www.princesspoppy.com

PLAYGROUND PRINCESS
A PICTURE CORGI BOOK 978 0 552 55603 3

First published in Great Britain by Picture Corgi,
an imprint of Random House Children's Books
A Random House Group Company

This edition published 2008

1 3 5 7 9 10 8 6 4 2

Text copyright © Janey Louise Jones, 2008
Illustrations copyright © Picture Corgi Books, 2008
Illustrations by Veronica Vasylenko
Design by Tracey Cunnell

Picture Corgi Books are published by Random House Children's Books,
61–63 Uxbridge Road, London W5 5SA
www.princesspoppy.com
www.kidsatrandomhouse.co.uk
www.rbooks.co.uk

Addresses for companies within The Random House Group Limited
can be found at: www.randomhouse.co.uk/offices.htm

THE RANDOM HOUSE GROUP Limited Reg. No. 954009

A CIP catalogue record for this book is available from the British Library.

Printed in China

Princess Poppy

Playground Princess

Written by Janey Louise Jones

PICTURE CORGI

To all my childhood friends
who are still my best friends
★

Playground Princess

featuring

Honey
★

Princess Poppy

Sweetpea
★

Mimosa
★

Miss Mallow
★

Abigail
★

Every day at break time Poppy and Honey played together.

"I so wish I was part of the Blossom Tree Club," sighed Poppy one day as she looked longingly towards some girls on the other side of the playground. "I bet they have way more fun than we do."

"But we have loads of fun," replied Honey.

"Let's go and play with them," suggested Poppy, ignoring her friend's reply.

Poppy headed towards the group of girls, which included Sweetpea, Mimosa and Abigail.

"Can we play?" asked Poppy.

"If you like," replied Mimosa, "but you've got to pass our test first."

"What do we have to do?" asked Poppy excitedly. She couldn't wait to be in their club.

"Come to Blossom Corner and we'll tell you," said Sweetpea.

Honey tagged along looking very nervous indeed, and when the Blossom Tree Club girls noticed this, they began to laugh.

"Ha, ha, poor Honey is worried about a little test," sneered one girl.

"We don't want the teacher's pet in our club anyway," jeered another, and everyone collapsed in fits of giggles except Poppy, who said nothing.

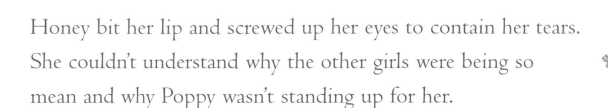

Honey bit her lip and screwed up her eyes to contain her tears.
She couldn't understand why the other girls were being so
mean and why Poppy wasn't standing up for her.

But she didn't have time to find out because Poppy's test
had begun. Honey stood to one side and watched . . .

Poppy was placed under the big cherry tree which was in full bloom. Then she was surrounded by the club members, who shook the branches of the tree hard.

"When you've been showered in petals, you'll officially be in our club!" explained Mimosa.

Soon Poppy's lilac and white striped school dress was covered in blossom.

"Your best friend is in now. You'll have no friends if you don't do the test, Honey," jeered Mimosa, as she swung from one of the branches. "Want to stand under the tree?"

Just as Honey was thinking that the test wasn't so bad after all, there was a loud cracking noise and the sound of glass shattering.

They had broken one of the branches of the beautiful tree and it had smashed into the greenhouse.

They all fell silent. Honey was quivering with shock. Mimosa
went bright pink and her mouth fell open with surprise.

"Don't tell on me, please!" she begged.

"Yeah, you'd better not or we'll never let you be in our club and you'll have no friends," said Sweetpea.

Poppy nodded in agreement even though she knew she should stick up for her friend and tell the truth.

Just then the bell went and they all headed back to class.

Miss Mallow was in a bad mood.

"I've just been told that someone has damaged the greenhouse and the blossom tree. Does anyone know anything about this?"

No one said a word, even though half the class knew what had happened.

"I *will* get to the bottom of this and I'll be very disappointed if I find out that any of you had anything to do with it," Miss Mallow said grimly. "Now, let's get on with class."

Miss Mallow got to the bottom of it sooner than the girls expected. It turned out that Bertie the gardener had seen everything. At lunch break, she called the Blossom Tree Club girls, including Poppy, into her office.

As punishment for the damage they'd caused they weren't allowed to hang around by the blossom tree anymore, and instead of jewellery-making they would have to weed the school vegetable patch for the rest of term.

The girls were furious and they were sure that Honey had told on them too.

After school Honey walked ahead towards Bumble Bee's Teashop. It had been a bad day and she couldn't wait to see her granny's friendly face.

"Tell-tale!" chanted the Blossom Tree Club as they caught up with her. "Teacher's pet! You're never going to be in our club now."

Poppy was very confused. She felt bad for Honey but she didn't want to be called nasty names and she really wanted to be in the club, so she put her head down and walked home as fast as she could.

For the next few days Honey
was called names at school,

and when she cried, the
girls just got nastier.

Honey simply couldn't understand why Poppy was still hanging around
with the Blossom Tree Club girls.

Until one day, when Poppy saw Honey sitting all on her own at break time looking so sad and lonely that Poppy couldn't stand it any longer. She had to speak up for her friend.

"Stop it!" she called out. "Stop picking on Honey. She hasn't done anything wrong. She's my best friend and I don't know why I even wanted to be in your silly club. Me and Honey have much more fun together than I ever had with you. I just hope she still wants to be my friend."

The Blossom Tree Club girls were shocked.

Mimosa stood open-mouthed. "You're no fun. You're out of the club!" she said.

"Fine!" said Poppy. "All your club does is mean stuff. I'm out."

Poppy said sorry and asked whether Honey still wanted to be her friend.
And although Honey agreed, she made Poppy promise never to be so
mean and nasty again.

Soon everything was back to normal.

Together they made a special den by the wild flower patch
and played at fairy princesses every break time.

Before long they'd both forgotten all about the Blossom Tree Club
and the problems it had caused between them.

Gradually, the petals fell from the cherry tree and the Blossom Tree Club was no more. One by one, the club members asked if they could play fairy princesses with Poppy and Honey.

"Well, if you want to be fairy princesses just like us, you've got to follow our rules," explained Poppy. "Number one, no tests; number two, don't ever call anyone nasty names; and number three, always tell the truth. Oh, and remember that Honey is the head fairy princess. Right?"

"Right!" chorused all the girls.

Honey smiled at Poppy. It was really nice having a special princess for a friend, even if she wasn't perfect all the time.